Congratulations on choosing the best in educational materials for your child. By selecting top-quality McGraw-Hill products, you can be assured that the concepts used in our books will reinforce and enhance the skills that are being taught in classrooms nationwide.

And what better way to get young readers excited than with Mercer Mayer's Little Critter, a character loved by children everywhere? Our First Readers offer simple and engaging stories about Little Critter that children can read on their own. Each level incorporates reading skills, colorful illustrations, and challenging activities.

Level 1 – The stories are simple and use repetitive language. Illustrations are highly supportive.
Level 2 - The stories begin to grow in complexity. Language is still repetitive, but it is mixed with more challenging vocabulary.
Level 3 - The stories are more complex. Sentences are longer and more varied.

To help your child make the most of this book, look at the first few pictures in the story and discuss what is happening. Ask your child to predict where the story is going. Then, once your child has read the story, have him or her review the word list and do the activities. This will reinforce vocabulary words from the story and build reading comprehension.

You are your child's first and most influential teacher. No one knows your child the way you do. Tailor your time together to reinforce a newly acquired skill or to overcome a temporary stumbling block. Praise your child's progress and ideas, take delight in his or her imagination, and most of all, enjoy your time together!

Library of Congress Cataloging-in-Publication Data

Mayer, Mercer, 1943-
    Helping mom / by Mercer Mayer.
        p. cm. – (First readers, skills and practice)
    Summary: Since Mom is sick, Little Critter tries extra hard to help get the house ready for Grandma and
Grandpa's visit. Includes activities.
    ISBN 1-57768-816-3
     [1. Helpfulness—Fiction.] I. Series.

PZ7.M462 He 2001
[E]—dc21   2001026662

McGraw-Hill
Children's Publishing

A Division of The McGraw·Hill Companies

Text Copyright © 2002 McGraw-Hill Children's Publishing.
Art Copyright © 2002 Mercer Mayer.

Send all inquiries to:
McGraw-Hill Children's Publishing
8787 Orion Place
Columbus, OH 43240-4027

Printed in the United States of America.

1-57768-816-3

1 2 3 4 5 6 7 8 9 10 PHXBK 06 05 04 03 02 01

 A Big Tuna Trading Company, LLC/J. R. Sansevere Book

FIRST READERS

Level **3**   Grades **1 - 2**

HELPING MOM

by Mercer Mayer

McGraw-Hill
Children's Publishing

Columbus, Ohio

Grandma and Grandpa are coming today!
I have to help Mom get ready. She feels sick.
Her nose is stuffy and her throat hurts.
"Don't worry, Mom," I say.
"I know just how to help."

5

First, I'll wash the dirty dishes.
We had a messy breakfast.
I'd better use extra soap.

7

Then, I'll water Mom's flowers.
They look thirsty.
I'll give them extra water.
I think I'll water the grass, too.

Next, I have to give Blue a bath.
He was playing in the mud again,
and he is very dirty.
I'll use extra doggy shampoo.

11

Now, Blue looks hungry.
I'll give him extra dog food.
Kitty is hungry, too.
I'll make her a special treat
with tuna and potato chips.

14

It's almost time for Grandma and
Grandpa to get here!
I'd better make some lunch.
I'll make peanut butter sandwiches
with extra jelly.
I'd better make lots of lemonade, too.

I hear a knock at the door.
It's Grandma and Grandpa!
I give them both a hug.

"Mom is sick," I say.
"I've been helping all day."
"You sure are a good helper,
Little Critter," says Grandpa.
"I sure am!" I say.

17

Word Lists

Read each word in the lists below. Then, find each word in the story. Now, make up a new sentence using the word. Say your sentence out loud.

Words I Know	Challenge Words
nose	today
dishes	stuffy
soap	throat
flowers	breakfast
water	extra
grass	dirty
jelly	shampoo
	thirsty
	hungry
	special

More Than One

A noun is a word that names an object. When you have more than one object, add an s to the noun.

flower ⟶ flowers

Add es to nouns that end in sh, ch, x, s, and z.

dish ⟶ dishes

Add s or es to the words below to make each word mean more than one.

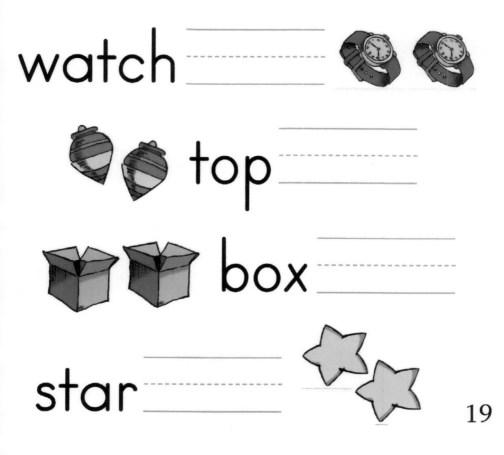

watch _____

top _____

box _____

star _____

19

Homophones

Homophones are words that sound the same but are spelled differently and mean different things. To, too, and two are homophones.

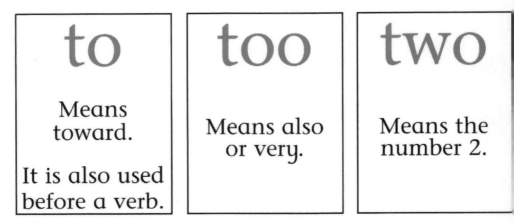

to	too	two
to	**too**	**two**
Means toward. It is also used before a verb.	Means also or very.	Means the number 2.

Examples:

to   Little Critter went to the pool.
            He likes to swim.

too   Little Sister went swimming, too.

two   They played for two hours.

Fill in the blanks below with to, too, or two.
The first one has been done for you.

1. One + one = ___two___

2. Let's go _____ the beach.

3. Little Critter is going outside to play. Little

   Sister wants to go, _____.

4. I need _____ eggs for the cake.

5. That soup is _____ hot.

6. We're going _____ eat lunch now.

7. Please read that book _____ me.

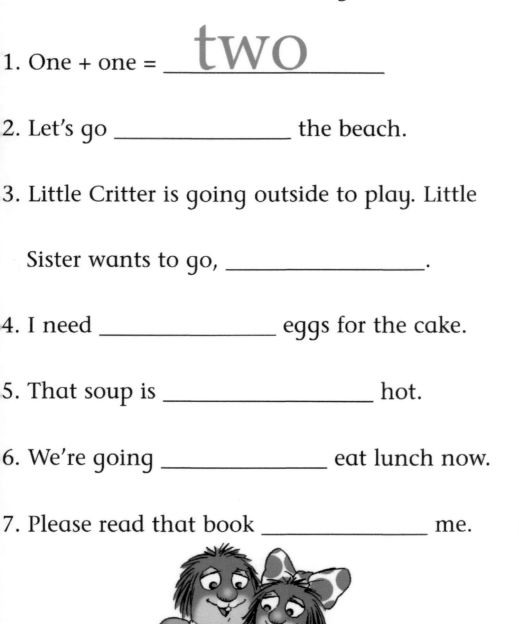

Show What You Know

The kn in the word know has an n sound.

Just remember: k + n = "n"

Write two words from the story that start with kn.

_____   _____

Read the clues. Then, write down the kn word that is described.

What you turn to open a door.

_____

You use this to butter your toast.

_____

The part of your leg that bends.

_____

He wears armor and rides a horse.

Making a List

List all the chores Little Critter did before Grandma and Grandpa came. Try to think of 6 things without looking back at the story. The first one has been done for you.

Things to Do Today

☑ wash dishes

☐ _____

☐ _____

☐ _____

☐ _____

☐ _____

Answer Key

page 19
More Than One

watch**es**

tops

boxes

stars

page 21
Homophones

1. One + one = **two**

2. Let's go **to** the beach.

3. Little Critter is going outside to play. Little Sister wants to go, **too**.

4. I need **two** eggs for the cake.

5. That soup is **too** hot.

6. We're going **to** eat lunch now.

7. Please read that book **to** me.

page 22
Show What You Know

know   **knock**

What you turn to open a door.
knob

You use this to butter your toast.
knife

The part of your leg that bends.
knee

He wears armor and rides a horse.
knight

page 23
Making a List
Answers may include:

Things to Do Today

☑ water flowers
☑ wash dog
☑ water grass
☑ make lunch
☑ feed dog
☑ feed cat
☑ make lemonade